B is for Baker Street

(My first Sherlock Holmes book)

Written by: Richard T. Ryan

Illustrated by: Sophia Asbury

Paperback ISBN 978-1-78705-639-8
ePub ISBN 978-1-78705-640-4
PDF ISBN 978-1-78705-641-1

Published in the UK by MX Publishing
335 Princess Park Manor, Royal Drive,
London, N11 3GX
www.mxpublishing.com

He lives there with Watson and Mrs Hudson, it's as simple as that.

C is for color.

Sherlock sees many hues, from silver to red to yellow, orange and blues.

E is for England,
The country of Sherlock's birth.
He thinks it is the greatest land
On the face of the Earth.

F is for footprint,
A very common clue.

Sometimes there were
so many, Holmes didn't
know what to do.

Holmes often pulled one out
When he was in a bind.

K is for knight.

Sherlock worked for many,
Sometimes they would pay him
Quite a pretty penny.

L is for London,
The city where Sherlock works.

R is for Railway,
Holmes often
used the train.

S is for Scotland Yard.
The detectives there
Would turn to Sherlock
When a case was too hard.

T is for Thames,
A river most important.
Many of Sherlock's cases
Take place near or on it.

X is part of examine,
What Sherlock does best.
He sees everything,
While others miss the rest.

Y is for year-book,
Sherlock kept a bunch.
Often he would turn to them
To try to prove a hunch.